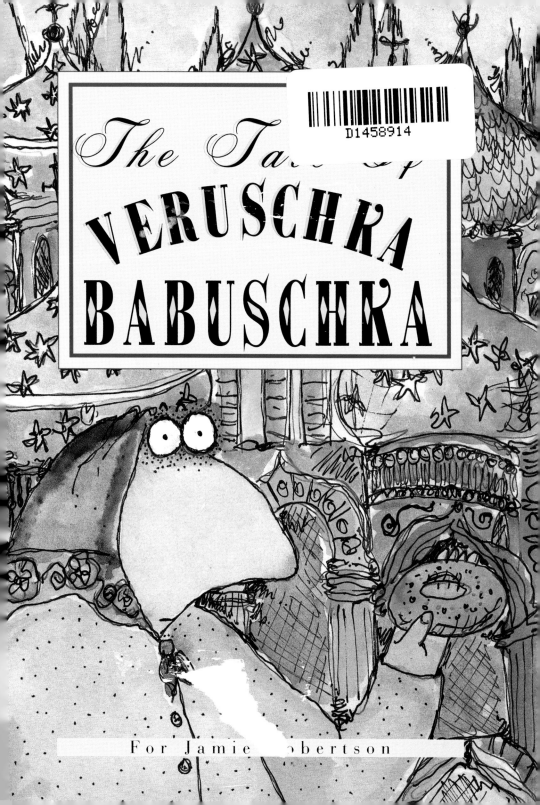

The Tale Of
VERUSCHKA
BABUSCHKA

For Jamie Robertson

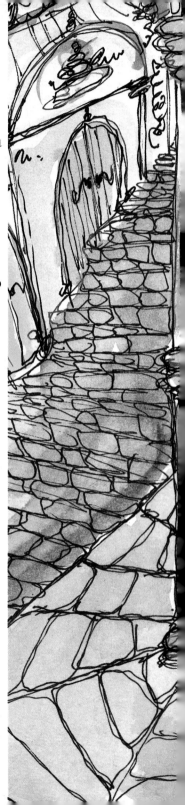

There once lived in the town of Trotsky a woman named Veruschka Babuschka, who was known by all to be a terrible gossip.

Nothing happened in Trotsky without Veruschka knowing, and no one was safe from her tale-telling tongue.

Every morning Veruschka Babuschka went shopping.

"Good morning, Bazel," she would say to the baker. "Let me have one big bagel, and let me tell you, I'm not one to gossip, but have you heard about Tizil, the tailor? Me, oh my! Just this morning he sewed his trousers shut and couldn't get dressed at all!"

"Is that so?" asked Bazel.

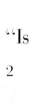

Next Veruschka would go to the cake shop.

"Good morning, Petruschka," she would say to the cake-maker. "Give me two pancakes, and let me tell you, they should be fresher than Bazel's bagels. I'm not one to talk, but he is selling day-old bagels for not a kopeck less. His mind is on other things, I think."

"Is that so?" blushed Petruschka.

"Would I lie about such a thing? Never!"

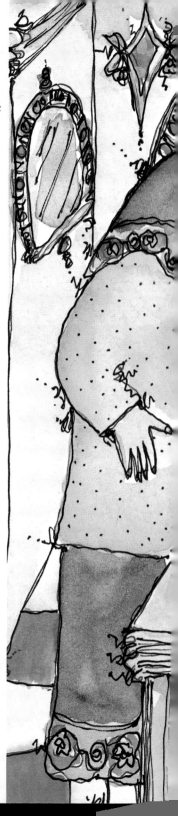

4

6

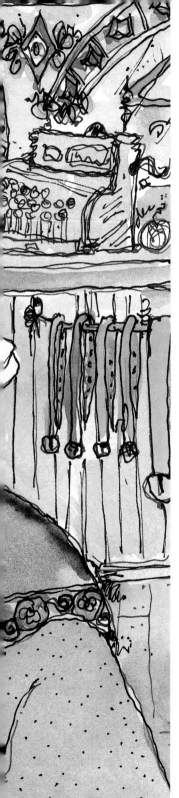

Last of all, Veruschka Babuschka would visit Golda, the sash-maker.

"Good morning, Golda. I have brought you a pancake. I'm not one to tell tales, but Petruschka's pancakes are as stale as Bazel's bagels. And speaking of Petruschka, have you seen her new dress? I'd say it was a gift from Bazel, the baker."

"Is that so?" asked Golda.

"Would I lie about such a thing? Never!"

And so it went, dawn to dusk, dusk to dawn, day after day after day. Veruschka's tongue never stopped wiggling and waggling and telling tales.

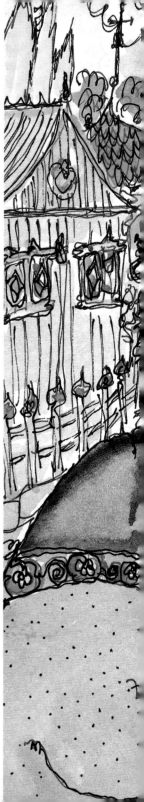

Then one morning as Veruschka was hurrying to the shops, she ran into Glinka, the doctor's wife.

"Good morning, Veruschka," she said. "And where might you be off to in such a rush?"

"Me, oh my!" panted Veruschka. "I was running to tell Golda what has happened. I'm not one to talk, but have you heard about the baker and the cake-maker? Such news! Such news!"

"Tsk, tsk, tsk. Such **gossip**!" scolded the doctor's wife. "My husband told me of a horrible disease gossips get."

"What is that?" asked Veruschka.

"Tsk, tsk, tsk," sighed Glinka, shaking her head. "It is even too terrible to talk about."

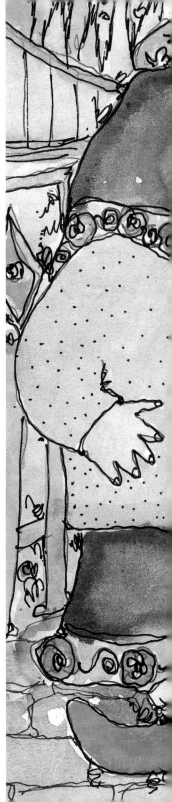

Veruschka put her hand on Glinka's arm. "You can trust me, Glinka. I won't tell a soul."

The doctor's wife looked up and down the street, then whispered in Veruschka's ear, "Gossips get foot-in-mouth disease."

"Me, oh my!" Veruschka gasped. "I should be so unfortunate to catch such a thing. And *speaking* of unfortunate, have you heard about poor Golda? Let me tell you. . ."

But Veruschka never finished, because as the doctor's wife walked away with her fingers in her ears, Veruschka's foot began to feel funny. Suddenly, it wiggled to the right. Then it waggled to the left.

"Stop, foot, stop!" cried Veruschka.

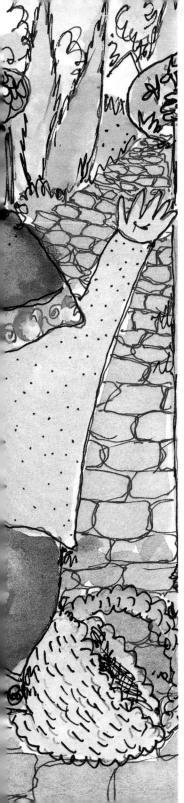

But her foot would not stop. And before Veruschka could say me, oh my, that foot flew up in the air and jumped right inside her mouth.

There it stuck, tight as a cork in a bottle. No matter how she tugged and pulled and yanked, her foot was in her mouth to stay.

It was Bazel, the baker, who found Veruschka hopping about with her foot in her mouth, yelling, "Melp! MMMELP!"

Tossing his basket of bagels in the air, Bazel ran as fast as he could to the cake shop. "Petruschka, have you heard? I'm not one to tell tales, but Veruschka Babuschka is dancing around town with her foot in her mouth!"

"Her foot in her mouth, did you say?" cried Petruschka. "I must tell Golda at once."

14

Out the door and down the street ran Petruschka,
yelling, "Golda! Golda! I'm not one to tell tales, but
have you heard?"

Soon the whole town of Trotsky was talking about
Veruschka, and before long a curious crowd gathered
around her.

"**M**MM! NLLL! FZZZT!" Veruschka wailed, as she tugged and tugged at her foot. Just then Pilovich, the doctor, pushed through the crowd. "So, Veruschka, you have finally caught it, have you?"

"MOOMF," said Veruschka sadly.

16

"Tsk, tsk, tsk. There is little I can do," said the doctor, shaking his head. "Getting a gossip's foot into the mouth is easy. But getting it out again? That is not so easy. I think, Veruschka, your foot will be stuck in your mouth for a long, long time."

Veruschka looked so forlorn that the doctor sat down. "However," he said, tugging his beard, "there is one thing we could try."

"WAZZ'T?"

"I will ask you four questions. To these you must give honest answers. For if you were to *say* one thing and *do* another — tsk, tsk, tsk, you would end up with both your feet stuck in your mouth forever. Do you agree?"

Veruschka nodded her head eagerly, so the doctor began. "Do you promise, Veruschka, never to talk about Tizil, the tailor, ever again?"

Veruschka thought about this. Slowly she nodded her head up and down. As she did, her little toe slipped out of her mouth and wiggled under her nose.

"Good," said the doctor. "Do you also promise never to gossip about Golda, the sash-maker?"

Veruschka nodded her head, and another toe slipped out into the sunshine.

"Next, do you promise to stop telling tales about the baker and the cake-maker?"

Again Veruschka promised, and again another toe, and then another toe, slipped out of her mouth. Now only her big toe was still stuck.

The doctor wiped his brow. "Last and most important of all, Veruschka, do you promise never to tell another tale about anyone else in Trotsky as long as you live?"

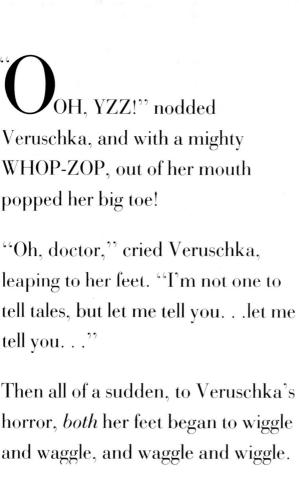

"OOH, YZZ!" nodded Veruschka, and with a mighty WHOP-ZOP, out of her mouth popped her big toe!

"Oh, doctor," cried Veruschka, leaping to her feet. "I'm not one to tell tales, but let me tell you. . .let me tell you. . ."

Then all of a sudden, to Veruschka's horror, *both* her feet began to wiggle and waggle, and waggle and wiggle.

"What were you saying?" asked the doctor.

Veruschka clapped her hands over her mouth. "Not a word," she whispered. "Not a word."

$\mathbf{A}$nd from that day on, if ever Veruschka Babuschka felt like telling a tale about anyone in Trotsky, she would quickly pop one of Bazel the baker's biggest bagels into her mouth instead.

And I'm not one to tell tales, but that is just how it happened. After all, would I lie about such a thing?